To the Tub

To the Tub

Peggy Perry Anderson

 sandpiper

Green Light Readers

Houghton Mifflin Harcourt

Boston   New York

The Library of Congress has cataloged the hardcover edition as follows:
Anderson, Peggy Perry.
To the tub/Peggy Perry Anderson
p.   cm.
Summary: Joe the frog needs a bath, but he makes the trip to the tub a challenge for his father.
[1. Frogs—Fiction. 2. Baths—Fiction. 3. Fathers and sons—Fiction.] I. Title.
PZ7.A54874To 1996
[E]-dc20 95-53267

ISBN: 978-0-395-77614-8 hardcover
ISBN: 978-0-547-85053-5 paperback

Manufactured in China
SCP 10 9 8 7 6 5 4 3 2 1

4500366479

To Brandon, Ariel, and Haley,
And their dad, Kurt

"To the tub," Joe's father said, "to wash the dirt away."

Joe said, "Okay.
But first hold my
boat and pail.
I will go and get
my whale."

"Come on, Joe,
to the tub you go."

Joe said, "Here is Ducky.
I want him. And I need
my ring to swim."

"Okay, Joe. It's
time to scrub your
spotted nose.
Time to clean
between
your toes."

"To the TUUUUUUUB!"

"Hey, Joe! Don't look surprised. It's time to wash behind your eyes!"

"Instead of dirty-green
and slimy, you'll be
squeaky-clean and shiny!"

"To the tub!"
Joe's father
said.

"We must wash away all the
dirty, icky goo you got into today."

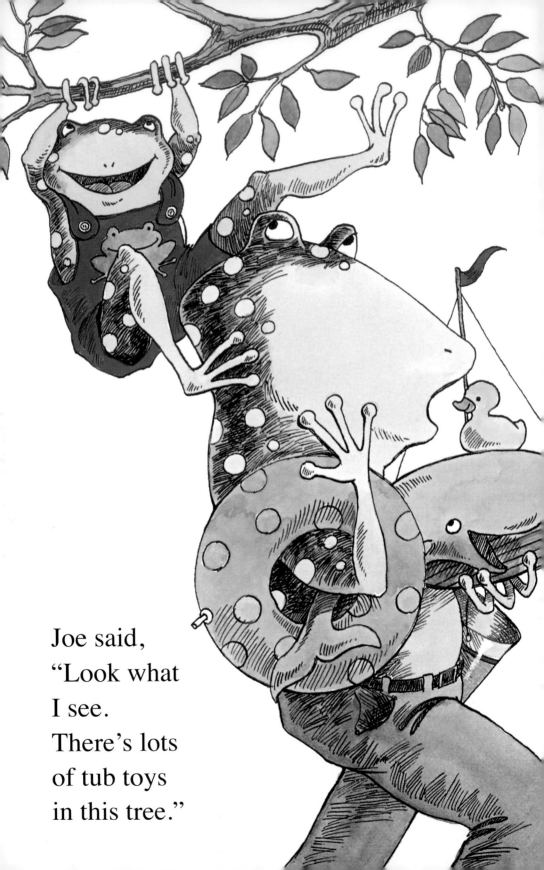

Joe said,
"Look what
I see.
There's lots
of tub toys
in this tree."

"Come down, Joe. Now that is all!"

"Just one more thing," Joe said,

"my big
beach ball!"

"To the TUUUUUUUB!"
Joe's father said.

"Oh, no," said Joe.

"Time for a . . .

MUD BATH!"

Hotdogs and Heroes

COLOSSIANS 4:6; TITUS 2:8a

Introduction:
God's Word makes it very clear how we are to live, but living according to the Word can also cause us some problems. We need to balance biblical principles to avoid trouble.

I. **Problem Faced**
   A. The Bible does not allow retaliation
   B. Some take advantage of that
      1. Ridicule and harass
      2. They hide behind rules
   C. Other teens think these "hotdogs" are "heroes"

II. **Problem Explored**
   A. Two kinds of people: the strong and the weak
   B. Two kinds of weak people
      1. The inept and incompetent
      2. The loudmouthed compensators
   C. Genuinely strong people do not say much about it — they just act
   D. This creates confusion
      1. Loudmouths appear strong, when they are actually weak
      2. The strong sometimes appear weak
   E. Undiscerning teens can not sort out the difference

III. **Problem Faced**
   A. To the "hotdogs"
      1. Your weakness is showing
      2. The Bible does not allow retaliation, but the strong might lose control!
   B. To the stronger
      1. Keep control
      2. Do not retaliate
   C. Others
      1. Do not make heroes out of "hotdogs"
      2. Do not be drawn to losers

Conclusion:

It takes some discernment to determine who is a "hot-dog" and who is a genuine hero. A little study of the Bible and some prayerful thought would go a long way toward helping you to tell the difference and avoid the trouble that can come from failing to discern.

When Things Go Badly

Introduction:
We all have bad days. It makes us feel a bit better when we observe that others have bad days as well, but that fact really does not do us any good. There are ways of handling them that can turn them into good days.

I. **Sense That God Is Speaking**
    A. May be punishment
    B. May be trying to get your attention
    C. May be trying to do something in your life
    D. May be trying to teach patience

II. **Ask God to Make His Message Clear**
    A. Spend time in prayer
    B. Spend time in His Word
    C. Seek counsel

III. **Be Willing to Learn**
    A. Act on what He shows
    B. Shorten the time of suffering by changing what needs changing

IV. **Do Not Run From Trouble**
    A. Literally — you can not get away from what God is doing
    B. Figuratively — by trying to quit, cop-out, blame-shift, etc.

V. **Let Trials Make You What You Should Be**
    A. No one ever became great without great trials
    B. Learn the lessons God has for you in them

Conclusion:
Even when things go badly, God is working in your situation. Look for the bright side, because what God does, makes, or allows has some good thing in it for you that you might miss if you do not look for it.

The Way of the Transgressor

PROVERBS 13:15

Introduction:
The Bible is a very realistic book. It not only points out how things should be, but it also clearly shows how things really are — sometimes other than they should be, as the teaching of this verse indicates.

I.   **Who Is the Transgressor?**
    A. Anyone who does things any way other than God's
    B. Includes many people
       1. The immoral person — in any manner
       2. The law breaker — especially of God's Law
       3. The rebel

II. **What Is the Hard Way?**
    A. It is already hard
    B. How is it hard?
       1. Uncomfortable
       2. Miserable
       3. Filled with problems
    C. Why is it hard?
       1. Because the person on it is not following directions
       2. God will not allow anything else
          a. He can not allow competition
          b. He wants each person in His way

III. **What Should Be Done?**
    A. We must recognize that no other way will work
    B. We must stop making excuses
       1. Poor self-concept
       2. Bad home environment
       3. Inadequate parents
       4. Other people lead me astray
    C. We must make a commitment to change

Conclusion:
God said it — I believe it. I will not try to do differently. Anyone who does lives dangerously, because, "He that hardeneth his neck . . ." He probably will not be killed; something worse will happen.

What Kind Are You?

1 THESSALONIANS 5:14

Introduction:
Most people have a very good idea of what a rebel is like and could probably spot one like that from a great distance. Unfortunately, not all rebels are typical. There are several kinds, and it is good to be able to recognize each of them.

I. **The Open, Hostile Rebel**
 A. He is the kind just described
 B. He is always recognized

II. **The Quiet Rebel**
 A. He never says much
 B. He resists by
  1. Refusing to act
  2. Failing to act

III. **The Passive Rebel ("chicken")**
 A. He does not really resist
 B. He does what is expected
  1. He has no heart in it
  2. He "bad mouths" it all the time he is doing it

IV. **The Conformist Rebel**
 A. He goes along with everything
 B. He rarely gets into trouble
  1. He hates every minute of it
  2. He builds up to blow-up (he is even capable of murder)

V. **The Vicarious Rebel**
 A. He does not show rebellion
 B. He is drawn to those who show rebellion
  1. He shows rebellion through others
  2. He is amused by others' rebellion

Conclusion:
Who is a rebel? A person who will not accept the authority of others in his life. Not all rebels, however, are open. There are many other kinds as well. What kind are you?

47

Authority

ROMANS 13:1

Introduction:
There are few things more difficult for most teens than taking orders from an authority of any kind. It just cuts against the grain of fleshly rebellion and youthful exuberance. It is, however, very important for teens to understand authority and its structure.

I.   **The Basis of Authority**
   A. God is sovereign
   B. He has established all lesser authorities
   C. He has given a "chain of command"

II. **The Nature of Authority**
   A. It covers all areas of life (God's will)
   B. It moves in specific chains
   C. It is designed to keep order
   D. It moves by progression through various stages

III. **The Reason for Authority**
   A. It prevents anarchy
   B. It allows older to lead on the basis of experience
   C. It restrains human rebellion
   D. It teaches us to submit to Him (as we submit to others)

IV. **The Limits of Authority**
   A. It stays within the confines of chain (your parents, mate, etc.)
   B. It is always limited by the Word of God
   C. Beyond those qualifications, it is always total
   D. You will never be called into account for obeying (unless you have violated a biblical principle in so doing)

Conclusion:
Every disobedience has a price in all of life. In everything we do we are sowing and reaping. How are you doing at sowing? It will determine what you reap in the future.

48

The Perils of Pauline
(or How to Survive in a Small Youth Group or Christian School)

Introduction:
Many Christian schools are small. Small schools have a number of problems all their own. Here are some tips for surviving in the small school.

I. **Mind Your Own Business**
   A. Allow others a personal life
   B. Do not ask too many questions

II. **Keep Your Own Counsel**
   A. Do not tell all you know
   B. Realize that what you tell others (even in confidence) will spread

III. **Stop the Gossip**
   A. Definition
      1. Things that are untrue
      2. Things are true, but
         a. Hurtful to the person
         b. None of your business
   B. Resolve not to be a carrier
   C. Reprove it in others

IV. **Get Your Feelings off Your Shoulder**
   A. Ask God for help
   B. Give your expectations to Him
   C. Grow up a bit

V. **Do Not Take Yourself Too Seriously**
   A. The world does not end with one disappointment
   B. You are not the center of the universe

VI. **Seek a Servant's Heart**
   A. Try to serve others
   B. This does not involve
      1. Probing someone's private life
      2. Trying to right their wrongs

Conclusion:

You can survive in a small Christian school (or any other small setting for that matter). In fact, you can actually benefit from it. You can grow up spiritually and emotionally. It is entirely up to you to determine what you will do.

Freedom

Introduction:
Everyone wants freedom. Something inside us seems to struggle for it. The tragedy is that teens often want something that really is not freedom, because they do not understand the real nature of freedom. Here are thoughts to help you to understand.

I.   **The Usual Approach to Freedom**
    A. Get rid of restraints (parents, authorities, government)
    B. Do your own thing (whatever you want, you can do)

II. **The Bible's Approach**
    A. "The truth shall make you free" (John 8:32)
      1. Statement of fact
      2. Truth is the real way to freedom
    B. We must know the truth
      1. Truth is the Bible (John 17:17)
      2. Knowing the Bible leads to knowing the truth
    C. Freedom comes by *knowing* the Bible
      1. Real knowledge involves action
      2. Knowing without doing involves folly and not freedom
    D. *Living* by the Bible leads to freedom

III. **The Logical Proof**
    A. Created products do not decide to "do their own thing"
    B. Things do not decide to be used for a purpose other than that for which there were created
    C. A train is most free, when it is running on its track

Conclusion:
Everyone wants to be free, but there is only one way to be free. You can do things God's way and know freedom, or you can do it your own way and live in bondage. Which course will you choose?

Things My Father Taught Me

PROVERBS 1:1-6

Introduction:
Most teens are not especially close to their parents. It is often the mature years that bring realization of just how much a parent was teaching during the growing-up years. Here is one adult's evaluation of the things his father taught him.

I.   **You Can Do Anything You Really Want to Do**
     A. Within human limits, of course
     B. "I'd give anything" — no, you would not
     C. We live within our own set of limitations

II. **If It's Worth Doing At All, It's Worth Doing Well**
     A. If we can not give something all we have, we should not be doing it
     B. The Christian should strive for excellence
     C. Ban the half-hearted and blast the mediocrity

III. **The Will of God Is the Most Important Thing in Life**
     A. There is no substitute for being where God wants you to be
     B. Do everything possible
         1. To discern His will
         2. To do His will

IV. **If the Bible Says It, Do It!**
     A. This assumes
         1. The inspiration of the Bible
         2. The authority of the Bible
     B. Does not allow for us to explain it away
     C. Biblical obedience is so crucial and yet so lacking

V.   **There Is Nothing Greater Than Salvation**
     A. Explain salvation
     B. It is absolutely essential because of eternity

Conclusion:
The things my father taught me seemed rather insignificant at the time, but they have helped me tremendously throughout life. Have you learned them yet?

Fatherly Advice

PROVERBS 4

Introduction:
This chapter is filled with small tidbits of instruction from a father to his son. The qualifications of the father to teach were given in verses 1-4. They are basically that he can teach his son because he, himself, was taught by a wise father.

I. **Get Wisdom and Understanding (vv. 5-9)**
    A. Key verse (v. 7)
        1. Wisdom is the most important and best thing to get
        2. Along with wisdom, be sure to get understanding
    B. Detailed benefits
        1. Preservations (v. 6)
            a. From folly
            b. From harm and danger
        2. Promotion (v. 8)
            a. Careful attention to wisdom will result in you becoming the kind of man who can be promoted
            b. Wisdom acted upon brings one to a place of honor
        3. Prosperity (v. 9)
            a. A crown of grace for your head
            b. A crown of glory on your life

II **Hear and Heed My Sayings (10-13; 20-22)**
    A. Key verse (v. 13)
        1. Grasp instruction in a way that it will not escape
        2. Keep hold of her, for she is crucial to life
    B. Benefits
        1. The years of your life shall be many (v. 10)
            a. You will avoid the errors that could cost you your life from illness or injury
            b. You will avoid things for which God might have to chasten you
        2. Your pathway will be unimpeded (v. 12)
            a. No hindrance in the pathway of life
            b. Even haste shall not be hindered

C. Background — the one teaching urges this, because he is sure his teaching is correct (v. 11)
D. Ramifications (vv. 20-22)
  1. Listen (v. 20)
  2. Heed (v. 21)
  3. Benefit (v. 22)

III. **Avoid the Way of the Wicked (vv. 14-19)**
A. Commandment (vv. 14, 15)
  1. Stay away from the wicked and the path they walk
  2. A strong statement in four-fold prohibition
B. Caution (vv. 16, 17)
  1. They find no rest unless they have done something to someone
  2. Even their bread and wine (the regular course of their lives) is tainted with violence
C. Contrast (vv. 18, 19)
  1. The path of the just grows brighter until it reaches the perfect day (v. 18)
  2. The way of the wicked is dark, becomes darker, and leads to an ultimate fall (v. 19)

IV. **Live Life Carefully (vv. 23-27)**
A. Keep thy heart (v. 23)
  1. Be diligent with thine heart
  2. The issues of life come out of your heart
B. Keep thy lips (v. 24)
  1. Put away a crooked (double-talking) mouth
  2. Put perverse (perverted) lips far from thee
C. Keep thy eyes (v. 25)
  1. Let them look straight before thee
  2. Make them refrain from looking at what they should not see
D. Keep thy feet (vv. 26, 27)
  1. Consider the places you allow your feet to go
  2. Make sure all your ways are thought out
  3. Do not turn aside from the proper path
  4. Keep out of the ways of evil

Conclusion:
Fatherly advice is offered in the interest of helping you. This is a tremendously, helpful chapter filled with the most practical of wisdom. A wise son will heed the instruction of a wise father.

The Perfect Crime

2 SAMUEL 11

Introduction:

If you like mystery stories, etc., you have run across the idea of the perfect crime. The ultimate perfect crime has not yet been invented, but there was a man who thought he had done so. We can learn so much from him.

I.   **The Study — 2 Samuel 11**
    A. David's lust is described (vv. 1-3)
    B. David's sin is described (vv. 4-5)
    C. David's cover is detailed (vv. 6-17)
      1. First attempt — (get Uriah to stay with his wife)
      2. Second attempt — (get him drunk)
      3. Third attempt — (pre-arranged murder)
    D. David's success — he got Uriah out of the way

II. **The Exposure**
    A. Only three people knew — none would talk
    B. God knew (last phrase of verse 27)
    C. God's revelation (2 Samuel 12)
      1. God told Nathan
      2. Nathan confronted David
      3. David condemned himself (vv. 5, 6)
    D. God's punishment is meted out

III. **The Lessons**
    A. You may do wrong and set up clever ways to hide it
    B. God always knows what you are doing
    C. God will deal with the matter
      1. He will expose you and your sin
      2. You will reap what you have sown

Conclusion:

There is no such thing as a perfect crime when it comes to God. Every crime has a witness — God Himself. Whatever secret sin you are harboring (and that is bothering you with its guilt), you might as well deal with it before God does.

Good to the Last Drop

PHILIPPIANS 3:13, 14

Introduction:
The time just before a goal is always a dangerous one. It is very hard to be in school during the spring; the last week on a job is very hard, etc. We need to be alert to the danger of any ending time, so that we can guard against the pitfalls that wait to catch us.

I. **What Is It?**
    The Tendency to Quit Before It Is Over
    A. Tempting factors — weather, weariness, love, etc.
    B. Forms it takes — grades, homework, jobs, etc.

II. **Why Is It Bad?**
    A. It can ruin much else
    B. It is usually the result of emotions getting in control
    C. It can influence future performance

III. **What Should We Do About It?**
    A. Go on as if nothing were happening
       1. Keep your mind on your work
       2. Do what needs to be done
    B. Finish everything you have to do

IV. **How Can I Help It?**
    A. Recognize it as a test of character
    B. Resolve to follow through
    C. Make completion your goal
    D. Start promptly to do what you have to do
       1. You can help others
       2. You can have free time later (do your work first — reward yourself for completion)
    E. Determine your own course (do not let others lead you)
    F. Take more interest in your work
    G. Do things one at a time

Conclusion:
It is ever so hard to "hang in there;" but it is really worth all the effort it takes. Do not lose for a few minutes, days or months what has taken so long to build and what will have such long-lasting results.

Look Out Below!!!

PROVERBS 16:18, 19

Introduction:
Teens have many problems: immorality, rock music, theft, profanity, rebellion, disobedience, etc. Which is the worst? Probably none of these. The worst is pride, and the Bible has a clear message concerning it.

I. **What Is Pride?**
   A. Excessive self-concern
   B. An excessively high impression of self
      1. Being impressed with your own importance
      2. Having a hang-up with your rights and how people treat you
   C. Thinking you are something when you are not
      1. Overstating your abilities in any area
      2. Assuming you do things well when really you do not

II. **What Causes It?**
   A. The "small pond" syndrome — you may be the best there is in your small situation but a nothing in a larger situation
   B. Your worshipful mommy and daddy who really think you are perfect — you know they do and work it for all you are worth
   C. A small amount of ability — can be deadly when you are the only one with ability in that area

III. **What Does It Do?**
   A. It blinds you — you do not see what you really are, and you do not see what you are doing and failing to do
   B. It makes you obnoxious — you get to be the kind of person others do not want to be around (either from haughtiness or from bragging)
   C. It destroys spiritual reality — you become a little, molded plastic figurine. You can not really see or know what God is trying to do in your life, because you are too busy with yourself

D. It sets you up for falls: God has a way of humiliating those whom He sees as being too proud. Watch for the fall — it is coming.

IV. What Can Be Done About It?
A. Recognize it — get help if you can not see
B. Confess it to God as sin
C. Pray for the Holy Spirit's help
D. Look at the entire Bible to see what you should be
E. Ask someone else to help you (someone more mature than you are). Do not just be what your mommy or daddy think you should be.

Conclusion:

Beware of pride, for it is deadly. Read Proverbs 8:13; 11:2; 13:10; 29:23.

You had better repent of your pride.

True Confession

Introduction:
The Bible calls for the confession of sin. This often bothers people, because it appears to be too easy. The truth of the matter is that it is too easy the way it is often done. Consider a number of types of confession and the motives behind them.

I. **"I Am Suffering the Consequences and Want Out"**
    A. Confession to get relieved
    B. This was the problem of Judas

II. **"I Do Not Want the Consequences"**
    A. I have done wrong
    B. I have done so knowing I could always ask for help

III. **"I Can Always Ask for Forgiveness"**
    A. I know I should not sin
    B. But I know God will forgive me

IV. **"I Need My Guilt Cared for"**
    A. It comes after sin
    B. I need to have my burden lifted

V. **"I Go Through the Motions"**
    A. I know I must confess
    B. I must get it over with ("Now I lay me down to sleep")

VI. **"I Will Do It God's Way"**
    A. Confession = seeing it God's way
       1. Admitting it as wrong
       2. Recognizing its harm
          a. To God
          b. To me
       3. Being ashamed (repenting)
       4. Determining to be done with it
       5. Replacing it with some positive thing
    B. Guaranteed to get results

Conclusion:

Each of us needs forgiveness — frequently. God is always interested in granting the forgiveness we need. It must be sought and found His way, or there is none.

Wise Guy Or Wise Man?

PROVERBS 1:5

Introduction:

There is one in every school group. He is a "know-it-all," a "smart mouth," a guy with an inflated attitude. An earlier generation said, "Are you wise or otherwise?" The Bible condemns a wise guy but commends a wise man. Which are you? What distinguishes a wise man?

I.   **"He Will Hear and Increase Learning"**
     (He is always learning from everyone and in all situations)
     A. Keeps his prejudices and presuppositions under control
     B. Listens to the viewpoints of others
     C. Learns from every situation
        1. What someone does better than he does
        2. The mistakes and poor examples of others
        3. His own mistakes and failures
     D. Seeks new avenues of learning
        1. Always listening
        2. Reading everything possible
        3. Asking questions

II. **"He Shall Attain Unto Wise Counsels"**
     (He seeks help from wise people)
     A. Obedience to the Bible
        1. Wisest of the Wise
        2. The "wise guy" will try to outsmart authorities at times, but he never will outsmart the Bible
     B. Turning to the Bible in times of trouble
     C. Seeking and accepting counsel from the right people
        1. Spiritual authorities
        2. Those who tell us what we need rather than what we want
     D. Learning from the lives of others

Conclusion:

The Bible makes it very plain how we can distinguish between the wise and the foolish man. We can tell what others are. We can tell what we are. Are you wise or otherwise?

The Ultimate Lie

Introduction:
Lying is a very common thing among teens. Almost everyone lies at times, but most would stop short of lying to God. The problem is that there are many ways in which we can lie to God, and it is very common to do so.

I.   **We Lie to God, When We Go Against What We Really Believe**
   A. We all believe certain things
   B. But our conduct is not always determined by our beliefs
      1. We do what we like or feel like
      2. We mentally adjust our beliefs
   C. Thus we are not true to ourselves
   D. A man who is not true to himself is not true to God

II. **We Lie to God, When We Go Against Our Commitments**
   A. We make great commitments
   B. Then we violate them
      1. We make them knowing we will break them
      2. We break them knowing we are doing so
   C. A man who is not true to his word is not true to his God

III. **We Lie to God, When We Accept What God Says and Then Do What We Want**
   A. We listen to teaching/preaching
   B. We raise no valid objection (based on the Word)
   C. We go and do what we want to do anyhow
   D. This involves setting our wills against God's
   E. A man who will not obey God's Word is not true to his God

Conclusion:
When it comes to truth, some teens have unspeakably bad records. A man who is not even true to himself will never amount to anything for God.

In the Days of Thy Youth

2 TIMOTHY 2:23; 1 TIMOTHY 4:12; ECCLESIASTES 12:1

Introduction:
The Bible is the oldest youth book and youngest old book. It speaks of young people: Samuel, David, Joseph and Daniel. It also speaks to young people. Let's see what is says to young people today.

I. **There Are Special Problems of Youth (2 Timothy 2:23)**
    A. Every age group has its special sins (detail some)
    B. Youth seems more prone to certain things
       1. Sins of action
       2. Sins of impetuosity
       3. Sins of inexperience
    C. Paul says to run away from them
       1. Joseph — the example
       2. You are to win!

II. **There Is a Special Potential in Youth (1 Timothy 4:12)**
    A. Do not let man look down on you as a youth
    B. Be an example to believers
       1. Reverses the usual trend
       2. It is possible for it is commanded
    C. Areas involved
       1. "Word" — what you say
       2. "Conversation" — your general conduct
       3. "Love" — the way you show what you are
       4. "Spirit" — not Holy Spirit — refers to your attitude
       5. "Faith" — belief in God's ability
       6. "Purity" — especially moral
          What kind of example are you?

III. **There Is a Special Challenge to Youth (Ecclesiastes 12:1)**
     A. Remember the Creator
        1. Hold God in mind
        2. Give attention to
           a. His will
           b. His glory
           c. His purposes

B. Remember Him *now*
1. While you are still young
2. At the present moment
C. Remember before it is too late and
1. Patterns are established
2. You reap what you have sown
3. Change becomes too difficult

Conclusion:

The teen years are such a crucial time, and the young adult years are equally important. Use them wisely. Get away from sin; establish a firm example; give attention to God and give Him the proper place in your life.

"To the tub," Joe's mother said.
"And please be neat.
Wipe your feet."